ON TOP OF OLD SMOKY

Retold by BLAKE HOENA

Illustrated by LUCY FLEMING

CANTATA
LEARNING

WWW.CANTATALEARNING.COM

CANTATA
LEARNING

Published by Cantata Learning
1710 Roe Crest Drive
North Mankato, MN 56003
www.cantatalearning.com

Library of Congress Control Number: 2015932814
Hoena, Blake
     On Top of Old Smoky / retold by Blake Hoena; Illustrated by Lucy Fleming
     Series: Tangled Tunes
     Audience: Ages: 3–8; Grades: PreK–3
     Summary: In this twist on the classic song "On Top of Old Smoky," a brave hunter
and his pet pig go in search of the legendary Bigfoot.
     ISBN: 978-1-63290-359-4 (library binding/CD)
     ISBN: 978-1-63290-490-4 (paperback/CD)
     ISBN: 978-1-63290-520-8 (paperback)
     1. Stories in rhymes. 2. Bigfoot—fiction. 3. Animals—fiction.

Book design, Tim Palin Creative
Editorial direction, Flat Sole Studio
Music direction, Elizabeth Draper
Music produced by Erik Koskinen and recorded at Real Phonic Studios

Printed in the United States of America in North Mankato, Minnesota.
122015   0326CGS16

Some people say there's a big hairy animal with large feet loose in the woods. They call him Bigfoot. But no one can find him. In this story, a boy and his **potbellied** hog go looking for Bigfoot.

To help them, turn the page and sing along!

On top of Old Smoky,
all covered with **fog**,
went looking for Bigfoot
with my potbellied hog.

We heard Bigfoot would **roam**
around collecting hats,
but all we could find was
a well-dressed **bobcat**.

Then we thought we saw him,
hidden under a **stump**,
but we were surprised by
a bad-smelling skunk.

On top of Old Smoky,
all covered with fog,
went looking for Bigfoot
with my potbellied hog.

We saw foxes and wolves,
wild turkeys and bears,
but none would dare tell us
about Bigfoot's **lair**.

So we looked high and low,
and side to side too,
but we could find no one
with **oversized** shoes.

Then one hot, rainy day,
the middle of June,
guess who jumped from behind
a bush and yelled, "BOO!"

On top of Old Smoky,
all covered with fog,
went looking for Bigfoot
with my potbellied hog.

SONG LYRICS
On Top of Old Smoky

On top of Old Smoky,
all covered with fog,
went looking for Bigfoot
with my potbellied hog.

We heard Bigfoot would roam
around collecting hats,
but all we could find was
a well-dressed bobcat.

Then we thought we saw him,
hidden under a stump,
but we were surprised by
a bad-smelling skunk.

On top of Old Smoky,
all covered with fog,
went looking for Bigfoot
with my potbellied hog.

We saw foxes and wolves,
wild turkeys and bears,
but none would dare tell us
about Bigfoot's lair.

So we looked high and low,
and side to side too,
but we could find no one
with oversized shoes.

Then one hot, rainy day,
the middle of June,
guess who jumped from behind
a bush and yelled, "BOO!"

On top of Old Smoky,
all covered with fog,
went looking for Bigfoot
with my potbellied hog.

On Top of Old Smoky

Americana
Erik Koskinen

1. On top of Old Smok - y, all cov - ered with fog, went look - ing for Big - foot with my pot - bel - lied hog.

Verse 2
We heard Bigfoot would roam
around collecting hats,
but all we could find was
a well-dressed bobcat.

Verse 3
Then we thought we saw him,
hidden under a stump,
but we were surprised by
a bad-smelling skunk.

Verse 4
On top of Old Smoky,
all covered with fog,
went looking for Bigfoot
with my potbellied hog.

Verse 5
We saw foxes and wolves,
wild turkeys and bears,
but none would dare tell us
about Bigfoot's lair.

Verse 6
So we looked high and low,
and side to side too,
but we could find no one
with oversized shoes.

Verse 7
Then one hot, rainy day,
the middle of June,
guess who jumped from behind
a bush and yelled, "BOO!"

Verse 8
On top of Old Smoky,
all covered with fog,
went looking for Bigfoot
with my potbellied hog.

GLOSSARY

bobcat—a spotted wildcat

fog—clouds close to the ground

lair—the resting place of a wild animal

oversized—larger than normal

potbellied—having a large belly that sticks out

roam—to go from place to place

stump—the part of a tree left when the tree is cut down

GUIDED READING ACTIVITIES

1. The boy and his hog are looking for Bigfoot. Have you ever heard of Bigfoot? Have you ever seen a potbellied pig?

2. The boy finds a bobcat. What is it wearing? What does the boy smell inside the stump?

3. No one has ever really seen Bigfoot. Draw a silly picture of what you think he might look like. Why is he called Bigfoot?

TO LEARN MORE

Burgan, Michael. *The Unsolved Mystery of Bigfoot*. North Mankato, MN: Capstone Press, 2013.

Michalak, Jamie. *So You Want to Catch Bigfoot?* Sommerville, MA: Candlewick Press, 2011.

Stafford, William. *Everyone Out Here Knows: A Big Foot Tale*. Portland, OR: Arnica Creative Services, 2013.

Troupe, Thomas Kingsley. *The Legend of Bigfoot*. North Mankato, MN: Picture Window Books, 2011.